Nile River Scorpion

Treasure Rebels Adventure Novella, Volume 1

Gerard Doris

Published by Gerard Doris, 2023.

This is a work of fiction. Similarities to real people, places, or events are entirely coincidental.

NILE RIVER SCORPION

First edition. September 29, 2023.

Copyright © 2023 Gerard Doris.

ISBN: 979-8215047620

Written by Gerard Doris.

Also by Gerard Doris

Treasure Rebels Adventure Novella
Nile River Scorpion
Congo Spider Fangs
Amazon Swamp Victory
India Yeti Pirates
Greek Gladiator Sharks

Standalone
Wrath of the Renegades

Watch for more at https://gerarddoristhrillers.com.

Table of Contents

PROLOGUE

(Egypt – Present Day)

The howl of a desert coyote echoed through the quiet streets of Cairo. It was midnight, and Africa's second most populous city was covered in soft moonlight. Twenty stories above the street a man in black looked down as the coyote's shriek reached his ears. He then quickly turned back to the glass and stone structure and pulled himself up to the thirtieth floor by using a complicated pulley system he had installed only ten minutes before.

He then began to quietly cut the glass, knowing he had turned off the alarm system eleven minutes earlier. The job complete he pocketed the special serrated blade into his black jacket and pushed the glass frame inward. The glass pane dropped onto the thick carpeted floor, making a screeching noise as it cracked in two. The man in black didn't care as he climbed inside. He knew the thirtieth floor study was built like a vault, a sound proof vault.

The study looked like a cross between a modern bachelor pad and the living quarters of a 19th century intellectual. Crimson red carpet from Turkey, modern steel covered tables and chairs, a French couch that looked as if it had been taken from Versailles, and wall to wall bookshelves packed with over a thousand volumes filled every corner of the room. Against the far wall was the electric fireplace, the artificial flames having been turned off hours before. Beside the only door was a keypad that glowed green to signify the door hadn't been breached.

The intruder walked to one of the bookshelves and swept the old tomes with blue light from his LED flashlight. He stopped and pulled an immense and ancient looking book off one of the shelves, two feet long by two feet wide.

He carefully laid the ancient volume on the coffee table and slowly opened the cover to reveal that the inside of the book had been cut out and a large brown package roughly one foot long and two feet wide had been placed in the centre. The brown paper was cracked and extremely old, held together with only a paper string. But once the thief undid the old string he could see that underneath the timeworn paper there was plenty of laminated protective fabric...wrapped tightly over a painting.

The man in black quickly retied the string and after pulling the package out of the ancient book he placed it inside the backpack he carried. He then left the book right on the table still open, and rushed back towards the window. He looked down at his watch and saw the digital numbers ticking down in the darkened room, realizing he had ten minutes before the alarm system came back on.

Quickly clipping his belt back onto the pulley system he then swung back out into the humid Cairo night.

Two storeys down everything began to go wrong.

Suddenly the thirtieth floor lights flashed on, followed by the ear piercing whine of the alarm. Automatically the lights from every other floor turned on until the entire apartment building was brightly lit. The thief turned his head and looked down at the street and his worst fears were confirmed. Ten Egyptian police officers who had been smoking casually three blocks away could be seen running towards the front of the apartment, their weapons drawn.

The thief quickly rappelled down until he was just two stories above ground. He then stopped and ran against the side of the building away from the main street until he was hidden by the shadows of the side alley. He lowered himself down even more until he was ten feet above ground. Unable to go any farther he unclipped the line and dropped onto the roof of a high end Land Rover. He smacked his knee badly but barely felt the pain as he rolled off the roof and dropped quietly into the dirt. He looked up and could see six more officers run past the alley towards the front of the building.

His original plan had involved rappelling towards an abandoned building on the opposite side and disappearing inside. But that was the direction from which most of the police were coming, and he would likely have never made it into the empty structure before being cut down by gunfire.

He looked at the Range Rover and scowled under his mask. Option two it was.

He pulled out the special serrated knife and cut a small hole in the door window. He replaced the knife inside his jacket, put his arm inside the window and pressed the unlock button. In total it took him only three seconds to break into the SUV.

He climbed inside and carefully placed the backpack in the passenger's seat. He hotwired the car and keeping the lights off he backed up towards the opposite end of the alley away from the main street. But before he reached the alley's exit three police appeared and the thief hit the brakes, causing the large car to briefly slide three feet in the alley mud.

The officers aimed their rifles and ordered the SUV to stop. The thief responded by putting the SUV in drive and crushing the accelerator under his foot. The soldiers responded to him by firing, tearing five holes in the Range Rover and shattering the rear window glass.

The thief didn't care. The SUV exploded out of the side alley onto the main street and he quickly turned right, pushing the eight cylinder engine over 110 mph. He looked in the rear view mirror and could see the street was filled with police lights around the building's entrance, but no car was in pursuit. He quickly turned down a couple streets, then after another minute of manic driving he looked back again. Still no police chase.

He turned down another street, then another, crossed a bridge over the Nile River, then after ten more minutes of manic driving he reached a poorly paved road with no large buildings on either side. He pushed the accelerator farther down and turned on the SUV's cold blue front lights. The desert approached.

The road continued to fade away until it was only a desert dirt path. The Range Rover was built for roads much harsher so the ride remained smooth. After twenty more minutes of driving Cairo faded in the distance, and soon the illuminated Great Sphinx and behind it the faint outline of the Great Pyramid became visible.

The thief didn't care to look at either of the two historically famous sites. He had a piece of history sitting next to him in the backpack.

He drove on for another two hours looking for a specific location. Eventually the SUV's blue lights illuminated a certain stretch of the Nile River in the distance ahead.

He pressed one button on his smartphone and holding it to his ear he waited ten seconds until a muffled voice answered anxiously. The thief responded with only two words: "Extraction now!!"

He didn't wait for a response but quickly ended the call and tossed the phone onto the seat. The blackened waters of the Nile River could be seen growing larger, and two miles downriver the faint lights of a small schooner could be seen approaching. The thief sighed in relief at the sight of the schooner and yelled out loud, "*I've made it*!"

Crack! Unexpectedly a bullet tore through the back window and ripped through the backpack before becoming lodged in the center console. The thief screamed in horror but before he could examine the backpack to see if the painting was hit, three more bullets shrieked past his head shattering the inside of the windshield.

Unable to see through the shattered glass he still continued forward, the SUV now completely lit up on the darkened path by police searchlights. The thief slowly began to lose control as he blindly hit a series of deep potholes which almost caused the Range Rover to crash. In moments the SUV was down to thirty miles an hour.

Two armoured police SUV's suddenly closed to within ten feet and they unleashed a volley of machine gun fire. The Range Rover was built to handle Mother Nature, not machine guns, and the bullets tore massive holes in the engine block and doors. The engine began to sputter and the thief knew it would die in seconds. The Cairo authorities called out for him to surrender, knowing they had him.

The thief instead looked out the shattered remains of the passenger window and could see the moonlit waters of the Nile

River only thirty feet away. He made his decision and spun the wheel.

The Range Rover roared towards the river, flying off the bank and crashing into the black water seven feet below. Shocked the Cairo authorities immediately turned off the path and parked at the river's edge, their searchlights aimed down onto the water below.

They could instantly see the Range Rover bobbing in the water partially overturned, covered in steam as the cool waters of the Nile met the destroyed and overheated engine block. Four Cairo police jumped in and swam towards the SUV. Cautiously they approached and peered inside. Looking up they shouted to the twenty men still on shore.

"He's escaped in the water!"

Immediately every police vehicle searchlight was directed away from the Range Rover and instead used to scan the river in a searching pattern.

Fifty feet away the thief resurfaced, his backpack tied on. Taking a deep breath he dove back down before he was spotted. He hated swimming and he hated the Nile River. He didn't need to read any more true life horror stories in the news to know that swimming in the Nile could be extremely dangerous.

He waited for a couple searchlights to pass overheard before he surfaced again. This time he tensely looked downriver to see if the schooner was still approaching. Would his accomplice still risk coming close to shore into the storm of police searchlights? Or would his friend leave him?

What he saw surprised and horrified him. The schooner was not coming close to shore, or leaving. Instead the schooner was surrounded by a ring of police boats and was being boarded.

As the thief continued watching the schooner in fear, a searchlight suddenly passed over him and the Cairo police began shooting into the air as they ordered him to surrender. He instead dove back down and the police began lowering small boats into the water to catch him.

The thief knew he was caught. The only question was, would he be caught with or without the treasure he carried? He looked around vainly but could only see blackness. At night the water was impossible to see through. He hated the thought of simply leaving the backpack behind. Who knows where it would drift with the current? Or worse, it might get buried in the Nile's mud, the treasure forever concealed.

Then he saw it through the gloom.

Almost a hundred feet away illuminated by a searchlight above was a wreck lying on the bottom of the Nile River. He instantly decided he would hide the treasure there. Quickly he swam towards the object, thrilled that the searchlight hadn't moved allowing him to see just enough to reach the wreck.

As he drew close he saw that it wasn't a ship but in fact a plane. A fighter plane. He correctly guessed it was from World War II and was German. Most of the plane was bent, rusted, or rotting. The pilot's seat beneath the cracked glass of the cockpit canopy was empty, no human remains. One wing was sticking up while the other was submerged in the mud, along with most of the plane's tail. The black swastika was almost completely faded along with the rest of the fighter plane's brown camouflage paint.

But as the thief swam nearer he could see something else was buried beside the plane. It was mostly concealed under the mud, and rested beside and under the wing that was also submerged in the river bottom. He didn't wait to examine it any closer, but he did see through the gloom the rusted outline of a ribbed iron track.

Almost out of air he turned back to the plane and could see a large tear in the plane's fuselage about three feet back from the pilot's seat. He quickly swam to it and looked inside, unable to see anything but black water and mud. He then carefully lowered the backpack inside and readied himself to swim for the surface.

But as he turned away from the plane he felt something brush against his foot. He turned to look down but couldn't see anything. But as he began to swim for the surface again he stopped frozen in shock as he saw something swim directly towards him, something that had come from inside the fighter plane. Before the creature reached him it suddenly turned and disappeared into the shadows of the Nile River's mud and weeds.

It had swum too quickly for him to get a clear look at it. But he had clearly seen a tail. A hideously long and strange looking tail. The paralyzing shock passed and was replaced with outright fear and he swam as fast as possible for the police boats visible overhead.

But before he reached the surface the creature reappeared and attacked him. The water became a churning froth as the thief spun in the water, flailing his arms to break away. He quickly pulled the special serrated knife out of his jacket and swung viciously to kill the animal. The serrated blade stuck into the river predator's back, and the animal temporarily turned away stunned, the blade still embedded in the creature's outer shell. Just as the thief began to think he was finally safe the creature sharply turned back with a flash of its tail and attacked him again, and in desperation he tried to pull the knife free.

But the blade wouldn't budge. The creature's large tail then recoiled back before shooting forward directly into the thief, the black bonelike barb at the end of the tail puncturing his backbone. Paralyzed the thief could no longer move or defend himself, and in moments his life was over.

(One Week Later – Private Airport – Outside Cairo)

"This heat is insane! Why must we wait out here?"

Randel King looked at his business partner and good friend, nervously finished the last of his iced tea, and finally responded, "Because Victor, I want to meet these people the moment they land."

Victor nodded and wiped his brow for the fiftieth time that day. They were standing near the tarmac of a single runway outside of Cairo in the desert. Behind them was a small air conditioned office, a large hanger containing five private jets, and a yellow black Rolls Royce Phantom with silver doors and roof idling beside the hanger.

As the Phantom and jets suggested, both men were wealthy. But the similarities stopped there. Victor was short, out of condition, and had made half a million by playing the stock market. Randel was tall, slim but athletic, and had made three billion dollars building one of the largest companies in the world. While Victor was dressed like a businessman on holiday, complete with the polo shirt, white shorts, and cheap straw hat, Randel instead was dressed like a man entering the boardroom, complete with the silk suit and polished shoes. Victor would have poked fun at anyone else for wearing a suit in the desert, but he knew Randel always wore his best when meeting important clients no matter the weather.

Instead he suddenly pointed to the blue sky. "Sir, there it is!"

Randel looked up and quickly spotted the private jet approaching. As he expectantly watched the plane descend towards the small runway, Victor continued speaking.

"I do not mean to dampen your enthusiasm, but I am certain that most of the stories about these people must be false."

Randel watched the luxury Gulfstream private jet coast onto the runway and glide to a slow perfect stop. As the plane's folding door opened and the air stairs slowly lowered to the ground, Randel turned to Victor and smiled for the first time. "You can't dampen my enthusiasm. You know why?"

"Why?"

As the air stairs smoothly met the tarmac and was secured, Randel took off his sunglasses and walked towards the jet saying, "Because every astounding story about these wild adventurers is true."

He stopped at the bottom of the stairs and waited patiently despite the searing heat of the sun reflecting off the tarmac. After the two stewardesses disembarked the only three passengers appeared and walked down the steps to greet him.

He knew from his research their names and accomplishments, but in person they were still a surprising sight.

The first was a man in his late twenties or early thirties. Travis Jagson. He was pushing six foot six in height, was a native of Hawaii, had short cropped dark hair, and had the relaxed easy going manner of someone who wasn't afraid of anything. Randel guessed that he spent all his time either underwater searching for treasure, or in the weight room adding to his 250 all muscle frame. Travis had been one of the country's highest rated boxers, gaining a perfect 40-0 record in amateur and professional fights. A shot at the heavyweight title was almost a certainty but two years prior he suddenly retired to instead hunt for treasure. He never gave any reason to the angry press or his bewildered fans. Randel didn't care what the reason was, because from what he had read Travis Jagson was an even better treasure hunter than a professional boxer.

Walking down the steps behind him was a young woman in her late twenties. Amber Monette. With her natural red hair, pink blouse, and white shorts she looked more like a French supermodel on vacation than a treasure hunter. Randel wasn't fooled. As a university student Amber had studied astrophysics and had an IQ of 150. After graduating she was quickly hired by NASA after which she spent a year helping to design a new space shuttle that could reach Mars. But like Travis she had suddenly switched careers without any explanation, leaving the space program in her words, "to search the beautiful world for unspeakable buried treasure." It was no surprise that her bright turquoise eyes reflected a wild and free soul, and not the shallow cheeriness of a model or the bland dullness of a mathematician.

Behind her was the unspoken leader of the small group. Maddox Tarver. The spikey blond haired adventurer's history was a mystery. No matter how much Randel had researched, Maddox's past seemed to have never been recorded. No family history, no academic background, no country of origin. The only details Randel could obtain referred to the past two years when Maddox along with the others had become famous after discovering gold from an ancient Greek shipwreck. Together they had discovered over eight million dollars worth of treasure from searching on three different continents. The media had given them the nickname, "Treasure Rebels" because of their unorthodox methods for finding treasure.

It was also clear from the newspaper clippings and web articles that Maddox had been the one to convince Travis and Amber to become treasure hunters, and that when he wasn't planning their next adventure he worked as a helicopter mechanic and enjoyed racing motorcycles professionally. That was all Randel King, or the rest of society, knew about him.

Therefore while it remained a mystery as to why Travis and Amber had left their public lives to search for treasure, Maddox himself remained something of a mystery to the public.

As they shook hands Randel could see that Maddox was slightly under six feet, had the appearance of a natural athlete, was roughly the same age as the others, and was wearing a Hawaiian shirt covered in drawings of sharks wearing cowboy hats. He also wore sunglasses that had an unusual looking copper tint. Unknown to Randel he had only taken them off while scuba diving for the last two months.

Because of Maddox's hipster appearance and the fun easygoing manner of all three young adventurers, Randel presumed the reason they hunted treasure in extreme climates was for some sort of adrenaline high. He couldn't have been more wrong.

With introductions complete they all turned to walk back towards the hanger but stopped as the Phantom limousine pulled onto the tarmac beside the plane with Victor grinning out the driver's side window. "To the apartment?"

Randel smiled and as he opened the passenger side door for his guests to climb inside he nodded his head and replied, "With haste Victor!"

PART I: CROCODILE WATERS

Three hours later the Phantom pulled up to the apartment building in Cairo that had been robbed one week earlier. The street around the main entrance had been roped off and police tape was tied across the alley entrance, the Range Rover's tire marks still visible in the dried mud.

"Use the underground parking Victor." "Aye."

Victor steered the limousine away from the main street and turned into another alley that lined the back entrance of the apartment. Three police officers calmly sat beside the only door which led to an inside stairwell. Victor slowed the car to a stop as all three men approached. He lowered the car's window and handed the lead officer a small notebook filled with I.D. papers saying simply, "The boss has brought his private team to search the apartment."

The officer looked inside and once seeing Randel immediately handed back the notebook. He then pulled a computer tablet out of a leather satchel tied to his waist and hurriedly tapped the screen a half dozen times. In three seconds part of the apartment's back wall slowly lifted to reveal a car garage hidden below the apartment's first floor.

With a smile from Victor and a wave of thanks from Randel the Phantom drove past the guards and disappeared down into the darkness of the car garage, leaving the bright midday sun of Cairo behind. As Victor parked in one of the few available spaces the garage "door" closed back into place above them.

Before Victor had put the car in park Maddox and Randel had already opened the two side doors. In moments the three adventurers were following the two businessmen towards a brightly lit elevator. The buttons and steel doors looked about a hundred years old, but when the doors quietly hissed open the elevator interior looked like something out of a modern New York penthouse.

As everyone stepped inside Travis couldn't help but smile and say to his friends, "Sweet ride to get here, but an even sweeter elevator!" Maddox and Amber just laughed.

The elevator rose quickly to the thirtieth floor. It stopped quietly, then after a dull ring the doors opened to reveal a plushly carpeted hallway with two doors on either side. Randel led the way to the second door on the left, quickly opening the lock by typing a key code into the electronic keypad. Instantly the green lights of the keypad turned blue then green again to signify the system was now unlocked. He then pushed the door open and let the others enter his apartment first.

The room looked almost the same as it had been when the thief left, except for police tape which covered the empty window space and a few more empty bookshelves. While Amber immediately began to examine the ancient book that still lay open on the table, Randel turned on the fireplace as Victor prepared coffee and iced tea.

Travis walked towards the empty windowpane and ignored the police tape as he looked out and down at the street below. He then examined the shards of broken glass that still remained on the carpet. Maddox instead simply stood in the centre of the room and studied every inch of the apartment while his eyes remained hidden behind the copper coloured sunglasses.

The billionaire stood quietly by the fireplace and waited for Maddox to ask any question. When none came he instead spoke.

"You are free to take your sunglasses off."

"I always keep em' on."

"Even indoors?"

"For now, yeah, even indoors."

"Alright."

Victor reappeared with the coffee and iced tea and the three adventurers were asked to sit down on the French couch. As Victor handed out the drinks Randel opened a large manila envelope and handed out five glossy pictures explaining, "A week ago a valuable piece of artwork was stolen from me in this very room. As you can see the thief came in through the window and took the artwork which I had hidden inside this ancient text. The artwork was drawn by a French artist named Miguel King during Napoleon's brief stay in Egypt. The painting itself does not depict any classic battles but instead that of a camel and jackal fighting amidst the sand dunes of the desert. The painting has been passed down through the generations, and that is how I obtained it as I am from Miguel King's family tree. The painting is one foot by two feet and in perfect condition. I would estimate its worth to be certainly priceless. Legend has it that it hung in Napoleon's private quarters while he stayed in this country."

He then took a sip of iced tea as the others examined the five photos of the painting. After a moment he continued, "The thief accidentally triggered another alarm here in the room when he didn't replace the book back onto the shelf. This led to the chase, which I know you must have read in the news reports. The chase ended at the Nile River where his accomplice and their getaway boat were seized. The thief was killed and his body was discovered the next day washed up on the riverbank. What wasn't reported to anyone was what happened to the painting.

The SUV was searched, including the entire route the thief drove from the apartment to the river's edge. I immediately hired a dozen scuba divers to search the river floor. I even asked them to use metal detectors. No painting discovered, only pieces of metal from the SUV which broke off after it hit the water."

Travis handed back the photos and said, "Is that how the thief died? When he crashed into the water?"

Randel nervously finished the rest of his drink then spoke again, "No. He was killed by crocodiles. When I said they found his body, I unfortunately only meant what the crocodiles didn't want."

"Have they identified through DNA testing who the thief was?"

"No Mr. Jagson. As we speak every criminal database in the world is being studied but I have been told it looks unlikely his identity will ever be known."

"What about his accomplice?"

"He only seems to speak Cantonese, and the authorities are having a hard time also identifying who he is."

Amber frowned, "So you have no leads at all?"

Victor then smiled broadly as he chimed in, "Yes we do!! Tell them about the Nazi fighter plane!"

Maddox's head immediately looked up in interest as Randel handed out more pictures and continued the story.

"As the divers kept searching for the painting they discovered the wreckage of a Nazi fighter plane submerged in the river muck, about twenty-five feet beneath the Nile's surface. You can see here in the photos that it appears to be a Messerschmitt Bf 109, one of the Nazi planes used during the North African campaign in World War II. No pilot was found inside and the cockpit was in extremely good condition. Much of the plane's tail is buried in the river mud but the midsection, propeller, and cockpit are still visible."

Maddox and the others studied the photos of the sunken fighter plane. Despite the brownish water the digital photos were exceptionally clear, and Maddox meticulously studied the interior of the empty cockpit.

Travis looked up from the photos and asked, "Any sign it crashed from an aerial dogfight?"

"The divers informed me that they couldn't find any evidence that the plane was ever shot down."

Maddox just smiled knowingly and without looking up said, "Gnarly."

Randel missed Maddox's comment and continued hesitantly, "But the divers did discover something. The plane is resting against the wreckage of some sort of vehicle that is almost completely buried in the mud. You can barely see it in the pictures. The divers began trying to clear the debris away to get an identification of the vehicle but they were interrupted by...crocodiles. Four or more to be exact. I'm sorry to report they attacked the divers with a fury. I am happy to say that no diver has yet died, but sadly one lost an arm, and two are still in critical condition.

"With three men in the hospital and two on life support, every diver has refused to return to the river. And while news of the crocodiles and plane hasn't reached the mainstream media, the diving community here in Cairo is close-knit and every man certified to scuba dive now knows of the danger. I even offered a million dollar reward to anyone who would recover the painting for me, but not one diver has shown any interest. I was forced to look for outside help, and because of your fame I immediately thought of hiring the three of you. Especially since you have experience swimming with dangerous animals. I also read about your adventures in the Pacific Ocean which thoroughly impressed me."

Travis set his photos down and replied quizzically, "I don't get it. The Nazi plane would be fun to study, but no matter how unique it is it isn't worth getting killed. Plus, you said yourself that the divers never found the painting on the river floor. So why do you want us?"

The billionaire grinned for the first time in minutes and replied, "I said they never found the painting on the river floor. But they did find the painting."

When all three adventurers looked at him questionably, Randel pointed to the photos.

"It's hidden inside the plane. Before the crocodiles attacked, one of the divers stuck the camera inside the cavity behind the cockpit in the plane's midsection. When the pictures were studied back on ship and magnified you can clearly see what appears to be a black backpack resting inside the guts of the plane. The thief must have placed the backpack inside after swimming free of the SUV, and after doing so he must have been attacked by one of the crocodiles before he could get away."

After studying the photo closely Travis still shook his head and said, "I admit your right, it looks definitely like a backpack or some sort of duffel bag. But the river water will have destroyed the painting. If anything the thief hid the painting in the SUV and what's in the backpack is just tools and other equipment he wanted to retrieve later."

"I assure you the police pulled every piece of the SUV apart and nothing was found, not even a fingerprint." Randel then walked over to the steel covered table and lifted up the now hollow book for them to see, "I kept the painting in this container which was made to look like a book. The painting itself was wrapped in special waterproof and lightproof material, then further wrapped in the original paper in which it was delivered to me. That painting could sit in the Nile River mud for a hundred years and still be in pristine condition."

As the billionaire turned to lower the book back onto the table he paused as Amber stated, "But that doesn't explain why the painting needed a book almost a foot thick to contain it."

Randel paused and for a split second was completely lost for words. He recovered and responded, "While the portrait is rather small and painted on regular canvas, its frame is immense and unique. It had something to do with matching Napoleon's décor I believe. At least that is the story that was passed down to me. The large frame is infused with gemstone which is why I asked the divers to use metal detectors. I was certain they couldn't miss."

He then curtly replaced the book back onto the shelf and turned back to face everyone while asking, "Are there any more questions, or can we begin to negotiate a price for hiring you?"

Maddox finally spoke and asked, "Why didn't you put the painting in a vault?"

"I consider my entire apartment to be a vault. Now that it has been broken into successfully I have moved all my other important possessions to another location."

Amber smiled and pointed to the bookcase where a dozen other "books" of various sizes had been removed, "More artwork?"

Randel simply replied, "Most of it, Miss Monette."

He then nodded to Victor who promptly laid a black steel briefcase onto the table. Victor then aimed a remote control at the briefcase as if it was a tv, and with the push of a button the briefcase lid popped open. He then turned the briefcase slowly around to face the adventurers while opening the lid the rest of the way.

He and Randel had used this dramatic demonstration a dozen times before and he expected the adventurers to stare spellbound at the thousands of green bills inside the steel case like everyone else they had tried to hire. But he was surprised to see that Maddox and Amber didn't even bother to look up, continuing to study the pictures of the fighter plane and painting instead. Travis also disregarded the briefcase, instead looking up at Randel questionably and asking, "Has anyone tried to break into your apartment before?"

The billionaire briefly sighed and motioned for Victor to close the briefcase as he replied, "No. But I understand what you are thinking. I do not know who the thief could have been, and to the best of my knowledge the thief had only one accomplice, who as you know is now in jail."

Travis kept his focus on the businessman and responded with another question, "So you guarantee that if we choose to help you we only have to worry about the crocodiles, not any vultures."

"Vultures?"

Maddox clarified without looking up, "It's just a name we give any criminals who will hurt, kill, and steal from others to get treasure. The world is full of vultures."

"As far as I know, no. Even the thief and his accomplice were never found to have any weapons stored in the SUV or boat."

A couple moments of silence passed as Travis and Amber both looked at Maddox who quietly continued studying the photos of the fighter plane. After another couple seconds he put the pictures down and nodded his head to his two best friends who grinned in agreement. Maddox then stood and shook hands with Randel.

"We're ready to negotiate that price Mr. King."

(Two Day Later – Nile River – Randel King's Private Yacht)

The three adventurers were sitting in chairs under a canopy umbrella on the private patio of the second deck aboard the billionaire's luxury yacht. Between them was a table littered with papers from their forty-eight hours of research and an open laptop. Maddox and Amber were wearing dive suits while Travis sported a simple t-shirt and track pants. They talked openly with one another, knowing they were out of the crew's earshot who worked below them on the main deck.

The yacht itself was over eighty feet long, painted black with a crimson red stripe, and featured a large mahogany lined main deck that sported a swimming pool and beach chairs. Today the artificial pool had been temporarily sealed over and the chairs removed to make the deck a proper place to work and prepare for a diving expedition. An open doorway led to the crew's quarters and mess hall, while a set of stairs led up to the second deck, which featured the private patio and the glass bridge where the yacht was steered.

As the crew worked on a strange looking cage that was attached to a small crane below them, Travis scratched the three day stubble on his chin and looked directly at his two best friends.

"I don't like pretty boy Mr. King. An' I know you two feel the same way. For all he knows every slimy art thief in Africa is after this little painting."

Amber closed the laptop and responded, "Vultures aren't the only thing he seems clueless about. I have little confidence the artefact he wants us to retrieve is the painting he describes, or that he knows anything about art in general."

"What do you mean?"

"I researched ever known art exhibit and historical site online and could find no trace or record of any painting of Miguel King's that came close to featuring a camel and jackal. I even contacted my friends at the Louvre and they confirmed they've never heard of the painting either."

Travis angrily spat, "So he's completely lying to us?"

Maddox shook his head. "I agree he isn't being real with us. But I don't think he's a criminal. I researched his family tree, and he really is related to the artist. I think our insecure friend Randel is a rich playboy who's too embarrassed and proud to tell us little commoners the true significance of what the thief took in the apartment."

Amber shook her head in disagreement and replied, "There is another problem. Remember how he confidently told us that gemstones could lead the divers to the painting because they were using metal detectors?"

"So?"

"Metal detectors don't pick up gemstones. He also didn't like me asking much about the paintings unusual width."

Maddox just grinned. "That's why you're diving to check it before we give it to him."

"There's more to worry about guys. His speech about crocodiles killing the thief wasn't exactly true either."

She picked up a small stack of papers and handed them to her friends.

Travis looked at the first page closely and replied, "This is the coroner's report I scanned yesterday, it says crocodiles clearly ate him."

"Turn to page three, it explains the crocodiles may have only eaten him, but didn't necessarily kill him."

Maddox and Travis looked at her questionably, "What??"

"His backbone was pierced by something strange, not a crocodile bite. The toxicology report goes further to say that his spine was filled with an unknown toxin. That's what really killed him."

"A rare type of poisonous jellyfish?"

"The poison is rare. But no known species could possibly pierce his backbone like that."

Maddox looked at the report in silence then at the cage being worked on.

Travis knew what his spikey haired friend was thinking. "You think Mr. King's special cage will keep whatever it is out?"

Maddox just smiled and put the report down. "You're forgetting I need to exit the cage."

Travis shook his head and chuckled. "You sure this dive is worth three million?"

"You both know why we're doing this." Maddox then paused and pointed to a small speedboat approaching the yacht with Victor and Randel at the helm before continuing, "And it's nothin' to do with Randel's money."

As the adventurer's climbed down onto the main deck, Randel's speedboat was quickly tied to the yacht. Still dressed in a silk suit and tie, he stepped aboard with Victor who was wearing the same polo shirt and shorts minus the straw hat. After greeting the five member crew they walked across the deck to speak with the Treasure Rebels who stood patiently beside the cage, the sun reflecting off its steel bars.

Randel removed his sunglasses and shook everyone's hand before pointing to the strange steel which lined the cage's bars.

"What do you think? The crew have nicknamed it the "animal cage." It cost a hundred thousand dollars but every greenback was worth it. The steel is of the highest production quality and includes the special trapdoor in the bottom you asked for. Between the main bars are two layers of bulletproof mesh to prevent crocodiles from swimming inside. There are also holes in the mesh large enough to provide you all with plenty of visibility without sacrificing safety. Also, instead of one cable cord there are four on the lid to help with stability while the cage is lowered and raised. Furthermore, due to the special hydraulic pulley system the crane can move the cage forward and backward underwater as well."

Travis grabbed two of the bars with both hands and tested the cage's strength. He then examined the unfamiliar mesh design closely and asked that the cage be lifted for them to see the trapdoor in action. The cage was slowly lifted five feet into the air after which one of the crewmen showed how the bottom of the cage could be opened and closed. After answering a couple questions from Amber and Travis, the crewman then closed the bottom of the cage and ordered the crane to lower it back onto the wooden deck.

After the crane had finished Travis looked at Randel and Victor with a big smile on his face, clearly impressed at the cage's design.

"It'll do Mr. King."

Turning away from the cage Maddox stared across the Nile and asked, "Are you sure we are directly over the plane?"

"Absolutely."

Randel then pointed at the shore a hundred feet to their right. "That is where the SUV crashed into the Nile, you can still see police tape up on the river bank. I was given the exact coordinates of the plane and my yacht is within a dozen feet of the spot give or take."

Following Randel's direction towards shore, Travis uneasily noticed that ten people stood on the river bank behind the police tape, watching the yacht with binoculars. "If it's still considered a crime scene how come so many people are here to watch?"

Victor beamed proudly and replied, "Randel is something of a celebrity. Those people can't know anything about the treasure, they are simply admiring us! This yacht always draws a crowd wherever it goes!"

Before Travis could reply Randel turned to Maddox and changed the topic.

"I understand you shipped in your own scuba gear and equipment. I have the finest dive gear in the world stored here on my yacht. All three of you are welcome to use anything you want!"

"You've read about our past adventures Mr. King. We only use our own equipment. No intended slight to you. It's how we roll when on a mission."

"I understand."

Maddox then pointed to Amber, "The two of us are going in the cage. Travis here will stay on deck and speak to us over the scuba intercoms. Please assist him if he needs anything."

"Certainly!"

While the five crewmen and Victor finished preparing the cage all three Rebels went below decks to prepare. Twenty minutes later they appeared back on deck with Maddox and Amber fully ready to dive. Both were wearing full scuba equipment including oxygen tanks, special digital dive masks with strange looking goggle rims, dive knives strapped to their legs, and underwater flashlights velcroed to their right shoulder. When Victor asked why the masks seemed unusually large, Amber explained that they doubled as emergency air containers that could last for five minutes or less, depending on how quickly the diver breathed.

But Maddox and Amber also carried equipment different from each other. His dive mask had a strange copper colour, and his dive suit contained two built in pockets behind his back. While one was empty, the other contained an odd looking machine about two feet long, with only the handle and red trigger visible. When one of the crewmen asked what it was he laughed and only said, "Just a cool little machine."

Amber instead carried a strange looking device that appeared to be a computer tablet but was three times as thick and featured a strange screen that glowed green.

Meanwhile Travis wore a simple headset and he positioned himself on a stool before a small table which was covered with audio equipment and an unusually large pair of black binoculars. He quickly explained to the crew that he could speak with Maddox and Amber who had intercoms placed inside their dive masks.

As the final checks were made by the crew, Randel stepped toward Travis by the console and pointed towards Maddox who stood near the cage beside Amber.

"I was wondering if you could tell me why Maddox always wears those sunglasses, and why he even wears a tinted dive mask?"

Travis stopped what he was doing and turned to look at the billionaire slightly annoyed.

"You'll have to ask him yourself when he resurfaces."

Randel wisely didn't press the matter any further and together with Victor and some of the crew they climbed the ladder to the patio above.

Showtime.

The "animal cage" was slowly lowered into the water where it bobbed back and forth in the calm greenish black surface. Amber climbed into the open hatch disappearing beneath the water. Maddox followed, giving Travis a thumbs up before closing the gate above him. Travis then turned and nodded to Victor who in turn signalled the crane operator to proceed. Within two seconds the crane's winch was activated and the cage began to descend into the depths of the Nile River.

As the cage slowly travelled downward Maddox and Amber strained to spot the plane but visibility was barely a dozen feet in every direction. The cable suddenly stopped moving as it automatically stopped a half-dozen feet above the river mud for safety.

"Do you see anything?"

"Nothing yet Travis. Move us forward twenty feet."

"Copy that."

The cage slowly began to move forward and the strange almost eerie sound of the cable moving was barely audible through the water. The cage stopped perfectly at twenty feet and Travis tapped his headphones once again.

"Do either of you see anything now? Randel is certain you are right near it."

Amber responded, "Visibility isn't too bad Travis, but we still don't see the plane."

Maddox suddenly said, "Move forward another ten feet."

"Copy that."

The cage hummed to life again, stopping in ten feet.

Suddenly Amber yelled in surprise as a crocodile brushed against the back of the cage, briefly rattling the steel bars. But Maddox didn't even care to turn and look.

"Travis, I got it man. Move us another ten feet forward and we'll be directly over the fuselage."

"Everybody good? I thought I heard a yell and the sensors read that the cage was just shaken."

Amber smiled beneath her mask and replied, "Just a crocodile Travis."

"Good! Nothing serious then!"

Travis then relayed Maddox's order and quickly the cage moved another ten feet. This time when it stopped the Nazi fighter plane lay directly below the cage, completely visible with no crocodile in sight.

Amber smiled again, "We got it Travis. No crocs to report."

Maddox and Amber quickly lifted the trapdoor on the bottom of the steel cage, and without hesitation Maddox then dove down and out into the open waters of the Nile. He carefully swam above the mud to avoid any chance of getting fatally stuck, and headed directly for the opening in the fighter plane's fuselage. To his surprise the backpack was partly visible, one of the straps was floating in the current a couple inches above the tear in the plane's midsection. Cautiously he examined the remains of the old plane, looking for any crocodiles or anything else that might seem unusual. Slowly he reached out and grasped the strap, and with a flick of his wrist pulled it towards himself. The black backpack easily pulled free amidst a flurry of sand. Maddox held the backpack close to his chest and slowly turned for the cage. He wasn't certain, but he couldn't shake the feeling that the disturbed sand hadn't been caused by him extracting the backpack, but instead by something moving inside the plane.

Ever slowly he swam back towards the cage, and content he was still alone in the water he handed the backpack up to Amber then swam back inside the cage, where together they locked the trapdoor back into place.

Amber immediately opened the backpack and pulled out the package containing the painting. They looked at each other in surprise. The package was torn near the center, a bullet hole clearly visible. But when Amber turned the package over there was no exit hole. The bullet was still inside. She quickly pulled out the tablet, secured it to the package and pressed a button. Instantly the tablet began scanning.

Maddox turned away and while looking back at the plane through the mesh he reported to Travis.

"Painting acquired, but don't tell Randel yet, he isn't going to be the happiest man alive when he sees it."

"Why?"

"Looks like Egypt's finest put a bullet through it when they were chasing the thief. Amber is scanning it right now. Can you still see the men on shore?"

"I'll check."

Travis turned away from the screens and picked up the extremely powerful black binoculars. Quickly he turned the lenses towards the direction of the shore, where far in the distance he could see the faintest outline of the pyramids amidst waves of heat from the desert. He quickly adjusted the binoculars for close range and aimed back toward the river's edge.

"All gone except two men...both on cell phones. Still looking at the yacht though."

A moment passed and then Maddox responded.

"What do you think?"

Travis wiped the perspiration out of his eyes, looked up at Randel and the others relaxing and eating in the shade of the second deck patio, then looked back at the men on shore.

"Victor's wrong. This yacht ain't that special. I would get back up here as soon as you can."

"I'm going to study the plane a little more as we discussed. Activate crane in about five minutes."

"Understood. Be safe my friend."

Maddox unlatched the trapdoor partway and flashed the okay sign to Amber who signalled back.

"How far is the scan?"

"Twenty-five percent finished."

"See you in under five."

Maddox then left the safety of the cage, and after closing the trapdoor behind him he headed towards the plane but this time he ignored the Messerschmitt's midsection and swam instead for the cracked glass of the cockpit. Some divers feel a chill as they approach any type of unusual submerged wreck, out of fear that they will find human remains. Maddox also felt a chill as he approached the cockpit, but not because he was afraid of finding any body. He felt fear because he knew who the Nazi was who had flown the plane decades earlier.

He grasped the cracked glass frame of the cockpit's canopy and with little effort he lifted the lid open. He looked inside, his heartbeat pace almost double. The pilot's seat was covered in mold and disintegrating, while the switches, dials, and stick were covered in grime. But due to the coolish waters of the Nile the cockpit had not completely rotted away. Maddox quickly pulled out his dive knife and began poking at some of the dials. He then reached down but froze just before his fingertips disappeared into the shadows underneath the seat.

He pulled his hand back, grasped the dive light and shined it under the seat. Sure enough, curled underneath the seat was a dark coloured snake. Maddox couldn't help but notice the irony and laughed a little. It seemed appropriate that since a human snake had occupied the cockpit years ago, now a reptile did.

Amber's voice suddenly crackled inside his headset.

"Maddox, two large crocodiles heading towards the tail of the plane."

Maddox didn't bother to answer. Instead he grasped the top of the seat with both hands and ripped the rotting metal seat right out of its sockets. The snake instantly exited the fighter plane and bumped right into Maddox's dive mask, which it instinctively bit. When both of its fangs broke upon impact with the reinforced mask, it immediately turned away in fear and disappeared into the green gloom, its body twisting back and forth as it swam away as fast as possible.

Already forgetting the snake Maddox quickly looked up and saw the two crocs were lazily circling the plane's tail, but coming no closer to him. He then shined the light back inside and began prying at the cockpit's rusted floor where the seat had rested. Nothing came loose except for small pieces of corroded metal which floated free of the plane as his knife scraped the steel.

Frustrated he set the seat back in its place then nervously he swam inside and sat down on the broken lopsided seat and began pulling and turning every lever and dial, even the ones that were completely corroded.

"Scan complete guys. It is the paining Randel described, but much more! It's...*MADDOX*!!"

Maddox looked up at Amber's warning and saw swimming towards him the largest crocodile he had ever seen. Instinctively he grasped the cockpit canopy and closed it shut just as the river predator reached the nose of the plane. The croc slowly continued forward until it was directly over the glass canopy, briefly casting a shadow over Maddox and the inside of the cockpit. As the seconds went by he estimated the creature's length until it finally passed and the faint light returned over the cockpit.

"Twenty-three feet!"

"What?! Are you okay?"

"I'm fine man."

He then returned to studying the cockpit but after another thirty seconds he punched the glass canopy in frustration.

"Nothing!!"

The intercom crackled as Amber asked, "Are you sure it's Wolfgang's plane?"

Maddox looked at the unusual gauges that had been modified decades earlier and replied, "It's his. No question. But there's no book!! Nothing!"

Travis then guessed, "Could the others have already picked it up?"

"No. No-one's been near this cockpit since the war ended."

Amber replied, "Keep looking! Travis, tell Randel to extend the time another five minutes!"

"On my way pretty girl."

Maddox sat quietly, his eyes studying every inch of the cockpit control panel. There was nothing left to try but the pilot's stick. But once he grasped the stick it disintegrated into multiple parts, including the button which fired the machine guns which floated away.

Discouraged even more Maddox stated, "It doesn't make sense! Wolfgang was a genius. He must have known the plane would corrode beyond recognition! He would have stored the book in a safer place..." He stopped talking as he spotted the ribbed iron track sticking out of the mud a couple feet away to the right and below the cockpit.

"I got something."

But as he turned to re-open the canopy he felt the entire plane suddenly shudder then stop. He looked up through the cracked glass but could see no crocodile in any direction.

"Amber, can you keep an eye on the plane's midsection where I pulled the backpack out?"

"Why? No crocs near."

"I think there's something living inside the plane."

"Oh."

He then quickly opened the canopy and in one smooth motion swung himself through the water onto the ribbed track sticking out of the mud beside the plane. On this side of the plane the faint sunlight was mostly blocked out, and Maddox was almost entirely in the dark. He grasped the flashlight, turned the switch to full power, and clicked the on button.

"Guys, I now know where he hid the book."

Beneath the beam of light resting in the mud of the Nile River was the rough outline of a World War II tank. Only part of the ribbed track Maddox was standing on, a dozen feet of the exterior left side of the tank, and a couple inches of the hatch were visible. The rest of the tank including the turret was buried in the black ooze, or hidden underneath the plane's hull. Maddox immediately swam up to the hatch and after re-attaching the flashlight to his suit he grasped the tank's lid and slowly began to lift it open...

"Emergency on deck!!! Two black speedboats headed our way, full of Vultures carrying Uzis!!"

"Comin' up!" Maddox replied as he closed the half open lid without having seen inside the tank's dark interior.

He swam up and over the fighter plane, not wasting a second to bother looking for crocodiles. He kicked powerfully and in moments he grasped the cold steel of the cage. Amber opened the trapdoor, Maddox swam up into the safety of the cage and the trapdoor was locked back in place.

"Pull us up Travis."

"Copy that!"

The pulley system immediately came back to life and the cage slowly headed for the Egyptian daylight above. Amber quickly showed Maddox the tablet her eyes full of excitement. "Can you believe what the tablet found in the painting!!??"

Maddox looked at the screen, the statistics and 3-D image surprising even him.

"Gnarly!"

Travis's voice interrupted them as they approached the final feet towards the surface.

"The speedboats are now circling the yacht. Randel looks like he's seen a ghost and Victor just lost his lunch. Did you get the book?"

"Negative. No time to finish the search."

The cage broke the water's surface a half minute later, but instead of stopping the crane continued pulling the cage upward until it was hanging twenty feet above the greenish black water. Amber and Maddox could see why the crane hadn't stopped the cage in time. On deck the entire crew, including Randel, Victor, and Travis, were standing in the centre of the deck surrounded by four men all wearing masks and carrying small Uzis. Standing near the hatchway thirty feet away from them were four other criminals all dressed in strange looking dive suits and scuba tanks. High above the deck the crane's cab was now empty, and the two black speedboats were tied up on either side of Randel's yacht.

Slowly two of the men in masks slowly walked to the edge of the rail and pointed their guns at the swinging cage which hung out over the water above them. Because of the mesh in-between the bars, the "Vultures" could not tell how many divers were inside. They called out for an answer but Maddox and Amber remained quiet.

Tired of waiting for a response one of the men turned and yelled in broken English at Randel, "Diver recover painting???"

Randel simply shook his head and refused to answer.

The thief grimaced and coughed fiercely, partly due to the unbearable heat under his mask, and partly due to his drug habit. He lifted his mask just enough to spit repeatedly onto the deck. Finally having cleared his throat he replaced the mask and pointed the Uzi at the crane. "Bring cage in."

But before one of the thieves could climb inside the crane's cabin, the lid at the top of the cage popped open and Maddox climbed out alone. Standing high above the yacht's deck he pulled off the dive mask and held the package containing the painting up for everyone to see. Confidently he yelled out, "Is this what you dudes want?"

The drug addict pointed at Maddox with one bony finger then at the deck below his feet. "You... come here."

Maddox laughed and replied, "No, I prefer crocodiles to vultures like you!"

And with that he replaced his mask and dove off the cage, painting package in hand, and disappeared into the River Nile far below with a roaring splash.

PART II: THE VULTURES

The thieves filled the water with gunfire but Maddox was already gone. He swam down furiously towards the plane and tank, turning the river around him into a white froth as his arms and legs churned through the water. He swam over the plane and dove down until his fins rested atop the tank's hatch. He knew he only had seconds before the thieves would spot him.

He grasped the hatch lid and even underwater could hear the hinges groan as he pulled it completely open for the first time in over seventy years. Holding the lid with one hand he reached for the light strapped across his shoulder, but to his surprise it was missing. He quickly guessed it had torn free when he dove off the cage. He looked up and could see in the distance the four divers headed directly for the plane, their own underwater lights piercing through the greenish water and resting on the Nazi fighter.

Without hesitation he swam into the darkness of the tank while he pulled the lid closed behind him.

As he locked the hatch he could feel his swim fins brushing against the Commander's chair in the darkness, and to his relief he realized there was no skeleton sitting there to greet him. With the lid now locked he turned to look around. The claustrophobically small space of the tank, full of water and in complete darkness, would have sent most people into a horrific state of panic.

Maddox never panicked.

Despite the flashlight having been lost he knew he would still be able to see. He lifted his hand and touched a small button atop the rim of his dive goggles three times. Instantly the entire rim illuminated with light, and Maddox could see the insides of the old tank.

Maddox was no expert on tank warfare but he immediately knew it was German made. At first glance there were no obvious signs of any cannon shells having breached the tank walls, and the corrosion inside from the freshwater seemed to be the only thing that had destroyed most of the switches and dials.

He swam down and hastily studied everything he could find. The long decades had corroded every piece of iron and steel, making identification of the tanks' different parts almost impossible. He looked down at what would have been the front of the tank, and saw protruding above the driver and gunner's chairs were bits and pieces of the fighter planes midsection. Clearly some of the tank's front shell had broken open, and when the tank was lowered into the river the plane had been directly placed against the tank's partial breach to keep it sealed.

Convinced now more than ever that the tank belonged to Wolfgang, Maddox swam back towards the top of the tank and sat in the Commander's chair to get a new perspective. He spun his head in every direction but nothing unusual appeared out of the gloom except for the broken pieces of a German Luger pistol that was floating in the water above the gunner's chair below him. Suddenly above his head the hatch began to rattle. The Vultures had found the tank.

Quickly he left the Commander's seat and swam back down to the gunner's chair, where the machine gun's handle still rested in place covered in black grime. He quickly examined the ancient gun and broken chair but turned away disappointed. No notebook.

Suddenly the hatch above stopped rattling, and Maddox quickly turned towards the driver's chair.

But just as he grasped the corroded chair a large Nile Catfish blasted from underneath the seat startled at Maddox's presence. The four foot fish swam straight for Maddox before cutting upward over his head until it accidentally swam directly into the Commander's seat with enough force to cause the rusted chair to slowly turn.

As the fish darted away towards one of the darkened corners, Maddox continuing to stare at the Commander's chair as it slowly turned in the white glow of his head light. There, barely tied to the back of the chair with rusted barbed wire was a small strange looking box about the size of a paperback novel, with a faint swastika etched on the box cover.

Maddox laughed inside the claustrophobic tank and spoke into the intercom.

"I got Wolfgang's notebook!!! How are things topside?"

Amber's voice replied from far above inside the cage.

"Still the same. One creep fired a couple rounds into the cage to make sure you were the only diver."

"Good thing for that bulletproof mesh and steel bars."

"Are you inside the plane? The four divers went overboard a few minutes ago, and the rest of them are waiting by the rails."

"I'm inside the tank. How's Travis?"

"He's trying to get back to the console to pick up the headset, but he can't get close yet."

"Can you signal him about the plan? I..."

Amber cut him off as she exclaimed, "Maddox! The divers just resurfaced! They're calling out to the others on deck...looks like they want something."

"How many are there?"

"Three Vultures. The other one must still be down there with you."

"I wish the crocodiles would say hello to him."

"They're giving the divers...what look like strange cutting torches! You have to get out of the tank!"

"You go ahead and take care of everything up there with Travis. I'll take care of the Vultures down here."

"Copy that."

On deck specialized and unique cutting torches were handed over the rails to the divers. Without a word the three thieves silently disappeared back into the Nile.

On deck the remaining four Vultures opened one of Randel's coolers and eagerly began drinking cold bottles of water. Forced to stand with the other prisoners, Travis moved as far to the side as he could without attracting the thieves' attention. But he was still twenty feet away from the intercom and headset. He knew Maddox and Amber would be talking and making some sort of plan.

Unable to speak with his friends he did the next best thing, which was to study his enemies and surroundings. By the way they carried their Uzis and took charge of the yacht and prisoners, Travis guessed they were mercenaries and not amateur criminals or traditional art thieves. They were also very controlled. No Vulture bothered to touch the plentiful gourmet food aboard, or to search the yacht for valuables to steal. They were here for the painting and nothing else. But he also noticed that the Vultures had become extremely agitated since Maddox had surprised them by jumping back into the river with the painting. Too agitated. They were in complete control of the yacht, and Maddox couldn't stay underwater forever. What could make them so fearful??

He then observed that the leader kept looking downriver away from the yacht every few moments. Travis slowly turned his head and began looking for any other boats in the yacht's vicinity. Sure enough in the distance was the faint shape of a police cruiser.

His attention downriver was broken when he noticed the cage's bottom trapdoor suddenly swing open. He watched as Amber quietly dropped out of the cage and disappeared with a small splash, never having been spotted by the thieves on deck.

Travis smiled to himself. Whatever Maddox and Amber's plan was, it was now in full motion.

Inside the tank Maddox placed the small box into the specialized pocket next to the painting, and he began to study the front wall of the tank which was pressed against the fighter plane. To his frustration wherever the tank's shell had been breached, each opening now covered by the plane was never bigger than half a foot. Even if he could force the plane free, he would never be able to swim through. Suddenly he looked up as the hatch began to shake as the Vultures tried again to pry it open.

After a few seconds the rattling stopped for good and an eerie silence followed. Then, a strange hissing sound echoed throughout the tank as a small red light appeared in the hatch and slowly began to move in a circular direction. The Vultures had begun to cut inside.

Topside Amber swiftly swam up to one of the black speedboats and after looking up to make sure no one was watching from the yacht's rail above, she then climbed inside the sleek twenty foot pleasure craft.

She grabbed a pair of binoculars off the seat and studied the Nile. Two miles ahead were three police cruisers slowly patrolling. Perfect.

She then smiled as she studied the onboard computer. The Vultures had gone with a state of the art speedboat, powered by batteries and a complicated and advanced computer system instead of a traditional gasoline engine and key start system. She quickly tapped the screen and using her incredible computer knowledge began to tamper with the battery settings. Quickly the batteries began to lose power and a few shut down completely. Satisfied the remaining batteries were close to dead, she then closed the screen and quietly slid back into the water.

Stealthily she swam under the yacht until her head poked above the water on the other side, her mask inches from the fibreglass hull of the other black speedboat. She quickly spoke into the intercom.

"Tank status?"

Maddox's voice crackled through her intercom.

"They're almost halfway in. Still working on my way out. Yacht status?"

"About to separate the Vultures."

"See you then in minutes."

"Copy that."

She swam towards the yacht ladder and silently climbed to the top. As she peered above the mahogany rail she caught the eye of Travis who was only a dozen feet ahead of her. She discreetly lifted both arms with two fingers showing on each hand. Travis nodded his head, immediately understanding the signal.

Two for you and two for me.

Amber quickly descended the stairs and jumped into the speedboat. She then began to tap the screen, this time not to tamper with the batteries but to bring this speedboat to life. After a couple seconds she turned away from the screen and pulled out her dive knife, slicing the rope holding the speedboat to the yacht in two. She then stepped back towards the wheel where she steadied herself, then grasping the throttle she pushed it swiftly yet smoothly forward.

The propellers tore into the water and the black speedboat roared away from the yacht leaving behind a tail spray twelve feet high. Just to make sure the Vultures noticed she then pressed the horn four times.

The thieves reacted exactly as she wanted.

Two of the Vultures immediately jumped overboard into the other speedboat to give chase. In seconds they were tearing across the Nile only a hundred feet behind her. Smiling underneath her mask she steered towards the two police yachts in the distance.

On the yacht Travis was finally unleashed. With four Vultures it was impossible to make a move. Now with only two he could fight back. The drug addict leader and the other remaining thief, who stood over seven feet tall, nervously stepped further apart to try their best at keeping the prisoners under watch. Travis waited for the leader to shift his attention for a second towards the chasing speedboats in the distance, and then he attacked.

Quickly grabbing a wrench lying on the deck, he then rolled five feet to the side of the monster Vulture and swung the tool down hard on the Uzi. The weapon cracked from the impact and flew from the criminals hand onto the deck where it slid right towards Randel King and the other prisoners. Immediately the billionaire rushed to grab the weapon.

Not even stunned the seven foot thief quickly pulled from behind his back a sick looking dagger, serrated and curved. He pointed the weapon at Travis and began to smile maliciously in an attempt to frighten him.

He never got the chance to complete the smile...hitting the yacht's deck unconscious after Travis' right hook broke his nose.

Travis quickly turned to see Randel and the gang's leader both frozen in place, five feet from one another, an Uzi pointed at the other's eyes. Everyone else on deck also stood frozen in place, terrified the wrong move would cause the Vulture to fire into them.

Randel stood coolly in place despite shaking a little from the adrenaline in his system. It was clear the way he was holding the weapon he had never fired a gun before, but the safety was off and Randel's eyes never left those of his enemy who stared back at him.

Without turning his head the drug addict called out to Travis in broken English to join the rest of the prisoners. Travis slowly walked towards the crew, carrying the serrated knife he had taken from the now unconscious thief behind his back.

Suddenly the screeching sound of sirens reached everyone's ears. The addict impulsively looked away for a split second to see that the two black speedboats were being circled by the Cairo police in the distance. Randel saw his opportunity and never paused as he pulled the Uzi's black trigger.

Click.

Randel stood still as he looked down at the gun, horrified and shocked it wouldn't fire.

Travis correctly guessed that the wrench had broken the Uzi when he had smashed it away from the other thief onto the deck.

The drug addict smiled and pulled the gun out of Randel's hands, who looked as if he had just been sentenced to death. With a sickening smile the addict then roughly tossed the Uzi across the deck against one of the rails and pointed his own gun at Randel's head.

"Goodbyee Pretteeboy!"

Travis threw the knife with everything he had.

The serrated blade spun perfectly and stuck directly into the centre of the addict's hand, pinning his hand to the Uzi. The addict lifted the gun instinctively in pain and the weapon fired harmlessly into the Egyptian sky. Before he could lower the gun Randel and everyone else leaped into action, piling onto the criminal and slamming him to the deck. Then having pinned his arm they separated his now bloody hand from the dagger and Uzi. The thief screamed out loud in fierce agony, but mostly in angry despair at knowing he was defeated.

With the deck finally now free of Vultures, Travis quickly ordered one of the crewmen who held the still working Uzi to watch the rail in case any of the divers resurfaced. He then rushed over to the other rail where Randel, Victor, and most of the others were looking in the distance at the speedboats and police cruisers.

Two miles away Amber finally slowed the boat to a crawl. Two hundred yards behind her the thieves' speedboat had suddenly died moments before, the depleted battery system having finally given out. The thieves began to fire their Uzis at her, but they quickly stopped and surrendered when they saw over a dozen officers pointing gun barrels at them from two of the police cruisers.

Amber cut all power and her speedboat slowed to a complete stop...ten feet from the last police cruiser which waited patiently for her to approach. Quickly a rope was thrown to her and the speedboat was tied to the much larger cruiser.

Nervously Amber slowly stepped towards the police boat holding both hands in the air to show she was unarmed. The police watched her every move, each officer's hand either resting on a gun barrel or holster.

She pointed back at the thieves in the distance and then at the handful of bullet holes in the speedboat's sides.

"See? They were the ones shooting at me!"

When they looked at her still not understanding she realized all they could hear were muffled words due to her dive mask. She had kept it on during the chase as the dive goggles protected her eyes from the spray, and she could continue communicating with Maddox.

Nervously she stepped forward and pulled the mask off, wondering how she would ever explain that she was the innocent party. She didn't have to worry.

The officers had rarely met any scuba divers in their life, and the only ones they had met were hardened aging men, going bald or sporting greyish beards. With the heavy scuba gear obscuring her buxom form, they presumed she would be just another male diver.

But once Amber removed her mask the officers were dumbfounded. With her shoulder length red hair, cheerful bright eyes and unbelievably pleasant smile, the men simply stared at her as if they thought she were some sort of goddess that had appeared out of the river.

When the officers continued staring, she broke the silence and pointed back at the bullet holes in the speedboat.

"See? I am the innocent one!"

She then pointed to the yacht in the distance. "Can you take me back to my friends in that yacht?"

The police immediately sprang into action, extremely happy to help her.

After one minute the police cruiser pulled up beside Randel's yacht and Amber impatiently was the first to hop aboard, even forgetting to bring her dive mask along with her. As the police began to interview Randel and place handcuffs on the drug addict, Amber raced to Travis' side by the intercom console table.

"Did Maddox resurface yet?"

Travis turned to her his eyes full of alarm.

"No. He just told me that the Vultures were about to punch through..."

He then ran to the yacht's rail and looked down at the blackish water of the Nile before continuing.

"Maddox's intercom just went absolutely dead!"

"Then we have to go down there!"

"I'll grab my dive equipment while you ask the police for help!"

But the top Officer in charge, a forty-something veteran who was a bit of a control freak, overheard them and stepping up quickly declared, "It is certainly too dangerous and unwise. I will not allow my own officers to dive, and if they cannot neither can you two. We will arrest the thieves when they resurface."

Before Travis and Amber could argue, the Officer had snapped his fingers and ordered his men to escort them away from the rail.

Far below the yacht Maddox desperately looked for an escape hatch inside the tank. When he had originally entered the tank he hadn't expected the Vultures to use torches to cut through the hatch, or that there wouldn't be any other means of escape. He had been certain there would be a hatch that would open out to the tank's exposed side above the river mud.

If an escape hatch did exist, he couldn't find it, as every latch and lever was sealed in place by seventy years of old grime. It had been a small miracle that he had been able to open and lock the tank hatch on top.

Above him the hatch was now nearly cut open, the glowing red light having almost cut a complete circle.

He had one minute left...at best.

Suddenly he pulled back in surprise as two more red lights appeared out of the dark, this time coming from the side of the tank which was sticking out of the mud. Maddox realized what the Vultures were doing. Diving into the tank was almost suicide for whoever dove in first through the hatch above, but if they could swim inside the tank from two different directions at once, Maddox would be much easier to kill or catch. They would wait to complete cutting an opening in the tank's side, then pour into the tank all at once from both directions.

He wondered why they hadn't started cutting the second opening sooner, then considered that the crocodiles may have been harassing them.

He swam forward one last time to examine the inside wall above the front seats to see if he could somehow pry or enlarge one of the gun sights, or pull free the wreckage of the plane's mid-section which stuck through.

As he searched his intercom suddenly beeped three times. It meant that Travis or Amber was trying to contact him, but he knew that the intercom signal had become too weak to work long ago.

The hissing above suddenly stopped and he looked to see the red light finally disappear. The Vultures were finished cutting the hatch. With a screech the cut piece of steel was pulled free and Maddox could see up and through the opening to the outside. No diver appeared, but the dark silhouette of a crocodile briefly passed over the opening. Meanwhile off to the side the two remaining torches had already cut half of a five foot square in the tank's side.

He finally gave up looking for an escape. He would have to fight. He drew the dive knife out of its sheath and positioned himself in the best spot for a fight. He had never killed a man before, but he had been in multiple fights and won them all, some even underwater. He was willing to hand over the painting but he knew the type of men these criminals were...they wouldn't simply take the artwork and leave, they would make sure Maddox never left the tank as well.

He kept breathing and refused to let any panic cloud his mind. He wasn't just fighting for his own life, but also for those who would die if Wolfgang's notebook never saw the light of day.

Then everything changed. The Vultures stopped cutting and a strange quiet followed. Maddox tensed, wondering if they might try to surprise him by swimming through the open hatch right now. He tapped the dive goggles and his light went out. Having been inside the tank for about fifteen minutes he had become accustomed to the cramped environment and would have the advantage fighting in the dark.

But instead of the Vultures pouring inside, the stillness was broken by a strange grating sound, followed by a slight rattling which reverberated through the tank. Maddox quickly tapped the goggle lights back to life and turned to face the direction of where the sound came from...the fighter plane.

Stuck in the mud and weighing tons, almost nothing on earth could move the tank. But the plane's midsection which was now partially inside the damaged front of the tank was shaking and causing the already damaged and ripped steel of the tank to groan in protest.

The Vultures must have also heard it and had stopped to inspect the plane.

Then unexpectedly the twisted front panel above the driver's chair shifted as a piece of the plane's midsection pulled free. Pieces of metal and other debris floated in every direction as if an imaginary mortar shell had suddenly hit.

But the light from Maddox's goggles pierced through the muck to reveal the impossible...Maddox's escape.

Somehow the plane had shifted causing five feet of the damaged front of the tank to collapse above the driver's seat, leaving only the damaged shell of the fighter plane visible. Maddox grinned triumphantly and with one hand pulled the "cool little machine" from behind his back as he thought, *There's nothing I love more than an underwater chainsaw*!

Underwater chainsaws were somewhat rare, and powered by pneumatic or hydraulic power, since battery or gasoline chainsaws could never work underwater. The version Maddox carried was specially designed just for him and driven by a unique power source. There were only three chainsaws like it in the world, and Travis and Amber owned the other two. The chainsaw would never been able to cut through the tank's heavy steel and iron, but the already damaged hull of a Messerschmitt Bf 109 was perfect to slice through.

The rattling in the plane finally stopped and the Vultures returned to the tank's side and continued cutting.

With a quick look up to make sure the hatch opening was still clear, and with the tank slowly filling with floating red embers from the Jackals' torches, Maddox pressed the chainsaw's red trigger and began cutting his way to freedom.

PART III: THE SCORPION

The chainsaw cut through the plane's corroded hull with ease, the spurred chain chewing everything it came into contact with. The chainsaw was surprisingly quiet and the humming sounds it did create were unperceivable to the Vultures who could only hear the sizzling hiss of their torches at work.

Maddox knew that something was living inside the plane; nothing else could have made the plane shake like that. He remembered how the plane had shaken earlier when he had been sitting in the pilot's seat. He wondered if it was a massive crocodile, perhaps a male that was defending its territory?

He then thought back to Amber's description of the toxicology report and the art thief's strange death. Could the creature that killed him be waiting on the other side?

He didn't stop cutting. Staying in the tank meant certain death at the hands of the Vultures. Escape by swimming through the plane meant possible death. Possible was better than certain.

Maddox finished cutting a three by two foot hole in the hull, the biggest cut he could make. He released the trigger and the chain quickly stopped rotating. He then placed it back in its holster and cautiously gripped both ends of the cut square, preparing himself to pull the sliced steel free.

Maddox looked up at the tank's hatch. Still clear. He then turned and saw the red torch lights suddenly disappear as the Vultures finished cutting in the tank's side.

Now or never.

Maddox pulled and the cut portion of the fighter plane came free, exposing the dark insides of the Messerschmitt Bf 109.

Maddox automatically pulled the dive knife out and swam inside. Unlike most aircraft a fighter plane's midsection was quite small but large enough for a man, or animal, to swim through.

Maddox headed directly for the tear in the hull on the other side of the plane and the open Nile River beyond it, but he never made it.

Out of the dark corner near the tail section a large creature burst forward and clasped a large claw around his leg, while at the same time the creature spun and swam through the cut opening...carrying Maddox back into the tank along with it.

As the creature pulled Maddox he slammed against the roof of the plane, tearing his backpack and holster off. As Maddox and the creature disappeared into the tank, the painting, notebook, and chainsaw silently floated to the ruins of the fighter plane's midsection.

Maddox spun and his light revealed a creature he had seen hundreds of times before, but on land and far smaller. Inches from his face and holding him in a tight grip with one of its claws was a strange looking six foot long scorpion, bluish black in colour, with a dozen legs in its midsection, and a powerful tail that pulled it through the water with surprising speed.

That very same moment the Vultures swam inside.

Chaos ensued in the small restricted space of the tank.

The Vultures immediately saw the scorpion and turned to escape, but two of the thieves were grasped by the scorpion's other claw before they could turn away in time. While the scorpion's stinger, at least a foot long, immediately sliced through the water towards the Vulture who had swum inside through the hatch above. But the stinger embedded into the Commander's chair before it could hit the terrified thief. The scorpion then tried to recoil the stinger but it wouldn't move, firmly stuck to the old chair.

Now distracted, the scorpion seemed to lose interest in the divers as it tried to pull the stinger free.

Maddox didn't hesitate and swung the dive knife for one of the scorpion's black eyes. The blade missed and scraped across the creature's tough shell atop its head, leaving a long scratch that the scorpion didn't even feel. Maddox lifted the blade to try again but the scorpion's claw whipped him back and forth and the dagger flew out of his hands, disappearing into one of the tank's darkened corners.

With the stinger still stuck, the first Vulture swam back up through the hatch and headed for the yacht above, while the other free Vulture turned on his torch and flashed it at the scorpion in an attempt to free his two friends.

The scorpion immediately released both the thieves in his right claw and Maddox in his left. With fury it turned and snapped at the torch, but it was obvious that the scorpion was somehow blinded by the red flame, and the mercenary crook easily hid from the claws while still flashing the torch.

Now free Maddox swam back into the plane and quickly pulled the chainsaw up and pressed the trigger all in one motion. With the saw-like chain now spinning he swam directly back at the scorpion. Whatever its shell was made of the chainsaw would cut through it. But as he re-entered the tank the scorpion thrashed and pulled the stinger free, ripping the Commander's chair right in half. Turning in a half circle its stinger recoiled...then flashed towards Maddox.

Maddox lifted the chainsaw up to his face to protect himself, and the stinger cut the chainsaw in two with ease. Shocked

Maddox watched as the chainsaw sank to the tank's floor now completely useless.

Seeing the tail begin to recoil for another strike he turned and swam back through the opening into the plane, just as the rest of the thieves swam for the side opening in the tank while the scorpion was still distracted by Maddox.

As Maddox entered the fighter plane he reached down to pick up the backpack with the painting and notebook inside, but gave up as he realized the scorpion was following him. He swam back out into the Nile with the creature's claws only a few feet behind him.

There was nowhere to hide now, and no weapon to fight back with.

With one push of a button Maddox released his air tank to be free of the added weight, and as the steel cylinder floated down onto the plane's exposed wing he swam furiously towards the yacht knowing every stroke had to be perfect.

He pushed himself harder than ever before, and he didn't waste a second to look back at the river predator. But as the yacht grew close he noticed only three of the thieves were near the surface and not four. He automatically turned to look back and saw the lifeless form of one of the Vultures in the scorpion's claws as the creature swam away in the now bloodied water. He guessed the thief had been too slow escaping from the tank, and that the scorpion had given up on Maddox and turned on the trailing thief instead.

Maddox broke the surface to a few cheers from the deck's yacht, but under his mask he wasn't smiling.

A ladder was lowered into the water and he climbed up onto the deck to see the scuba clad Vultures in handcuffs alongside the other members of the gang. Travis, Amber, Randel, Victor, and the Officer in charge immediately came over to see him.

Amber hugged him and Travis slapped him on the back saying,

"You always find a way to shock us!"

The Officer looked down at the water and back at Maddox questionably.

"There were four divers?"

Maddox nodded sombrely, "Yeah, the scorpion killed one of them."

The Officer and everyone else looked at him surprised.

Maddox didn't wait for their questions and continued, "A six foot scorpion. Amphibious. Never seen a creature like it, has a stinger that could cut through a car door. It completely overpowered everyone with ease. It's definitely what killed the Cairo thief."

Amber inquired, "Are we looking at a newly discovered species?"

Maddox replied, "Maybe...or one we thought was extinct."

Randel stepped forward and asked, "But everyone else here is all right?"

Maddox nodded his head, knowing what question would come next from the billionaire.

"And did you find the painting?"

Maddox was blunt.

"I had to leave the backpack and my scuba tank behind. The painting is still in the fighter plane."

Randel's eyes showed relief and anxiety at the same time.

"I'm glad you found it! Can this...scorpion be killed so we can retrieve it later today?"

Maddox began to answer but was cut off by the Officer.

"Of course not! Two people have been killed by this predator and anyone who goes in the water is at risk of dying as well! I will report this speedily to the proper authorities who in turn will take the necessary steps to trap or kill the creature and have it removed from the Nile."

Randel looked like someone who had won the lottery but just saw his ticket float away in the wind.

"But...Officer! I understand how long that process that will take! Weeks, probably months! I can't wait-"

The Officer aggressively put his hand up to Randel's face and disregarded his plea.

"Safety not artwork comes first. If it takes a year so be it."

Maddox, Amber, and Travis looked at one another with one thought on their minds.

The notebook.

Maddox stepped forward and asked graciously, "Officer, it would be unwise to leave the painting down for much longer. Even though it is wrapped in waterproof material, over time water may still seep in and ruin it. I'm sure we can retrieve it using the cage for safety."

Travis smiled and had already picked up a diving suit and scuba tank. "All three of us will go! We accept all risk and leave you legally free."

"No!! None of you are lawyers, and none of you are allowed back into the river." The Officer then snapped his fingers at a deputy who curtly stepped forward and briskly ripped the diving suit and tank out of Travis' hands.

The Officer then nodded goodbye and walking away he called out to his men to place the Vultures in the police boats and for the cage to be brought back onto the yacht's deck. Randel and Victor immediately trailed after the Officer trying their best to convince him to change his mind while leaving Maddox, Travis, and Amber alone by the yacht's rail.

Amber turned to her two best friends.

"The Officer is right to think the way he does. No-one should be allowed back into the river."

Travis sighed in agreement, "Especially considering he thinks it's just a stupid painting."

Maddox turned to Amber and pointed at Travis. "Did you tell him it's not really a painting Randel is after?"

Travis eyes broadened in surprise, "What?!"

Amber pulled the tablet computer out from under her arm and showed him the x-ray style image of the painting she took inside the cage.

Travis looked up from the screen and laughed, "I thought ol' Randy was more on the artistic side, not a military buff!"

Amber put the special tablet back under her arm and replied, "Randel may simply want them because of their age. The computer said they're partly made of material that is thousands of years old. They're probably so delicate they would just crumble if exposed to water or daylight."

A few moments passed as all three reflected on what was most important, while on the deck the cage was slowly lowered and secured.

Travis broke the silence. "If we don't get that book in time everything we've worked for will be gone."

Maddox replied, "No man, everyone we love will be gone."

Maddox then turned and gripping the steel rail he looked out across the Nile, ignorant of the incredible beauty which was visible in all directions. Instead he could only think about what he knew lay beneath the Nile's surface.

Still lost in thought he turned back and suddenly spied the torches which the thieves had used, lined up against one of the far rails. It was clear that the police were going to take them for evidence.

Amber put her hand on Maddox's shoulder and said, "We'll find another way to get the notebook. Maybe the scorpion will be killed quickly, or someone higher up in the police will grant us access."

Maddox kept staring at the torches and replied without turning, "If they won't accommodate a billionaire like Randel, they'll never make an exception for us."

Amber's soft eyes took on a look of dread.

"You said yourself its tail could cut through a car door. You can't outwit a brutish creature like that."

Maddox didn't respond and instead he walked over to the rail and calmly picked up one of the torches before any of the police spotted him. He then jogged back to his friends, torch in one hand and his dive mask in the other. He then stood with his back to the rail between Amber and Travis, and pretended to examine the torch when the Officer suddenly returned and inquired angrily what he was doing with "evidence."

Maddox looked up and grinned, "I'm just studying it. It's incredibly rare and worth over a thousand dollars! You don't see em' very often ya know."

The Officer didn't flinch and responded, "Return that to my subordinates. And if I were you I'd get changed into comfortable civilian clothes. You don't want to spend an entire evening in your dive suit answering questions for my supervisors. I've instructed Randel King to have this yacht follow our boats to shore in a matter of moments."

He then paused as if an unsettling thought just occurred to him, "You do understand that you *CANNOT* return to the water...yes???"

Maddox grinned even more, "I can't dive without my scuba tank!"

The Officer laughed in agreement, satisfied the matter was settled as he walked away towards the opposite end of the yacht.

Had he turned around once to look behind, he would have seen Maddox put on the dive mask, take Amber's dive knife without her knowing, and jump backwards over the rail, disappearing into the Nile one final time.

===

Maddox hit the water in full stride and headed straight down towards the fighter plane. No sign of the scorpion yet.

He reached the side of the plane and after resting the torch against the wing, he quickly scooped up the oxygen tank and reattached it to his suit and dive mask. He then reached down and pulled Amber's dive knife out of his leg sheath with one hand, while he grabbed the torch and pressed the trigger with the other.

Instantly a large red flame shot from the torch's nozzle giving the water around him a strange reddish tint. He hoped the torch would still blind the scorpion as it had done before.

This was it.

He dove inside the plane, torch first.

The plane's insides were empty except for the backpack which lay undisturbed in the twisted metal of the plane's midsection. He didn't bother to look through the opening into the tank, instead he pointed the torch's flame at the opening, re-sheathed the knife, then lifted up the backpack and clinched it back into place on his back.

As he began to turn...the scorpion struck.

The predator appeared not from inside the tank but from outside the plane, and in one motion its tail recoiled and then sprung through the plane's opening directly into Maddox's back.

The primordial black barb sliced through the oxygen tank, then carved through the painting before suddenly stopping. Maddox grunted in shock as his body was violently jolted forward by the force of the blow. The scorpion's primal weapon pulled back for another strike as Maddox flew forward until he was halfway into the tank, the torch having flown from his hand.

He felt deeper pain than he had ever thought possible through his back, while the water around him was engulfed with bubbles as the oxygen escaped from the punctured cylindrical tank. He spun forward and pulled his feet towards himself into the Nazi tank as the stinger appeared again, missing his fins and instead slicing more of the plane's steel midsection above the opening between the plane and tank.

Maddox released the tank underneath the backpack, and shoved the oxygen canister back threw the opening into the plane at the scorpion. The pain in his back was suddenly gone as life-saving adrenaline rushed through his body. He then tapped the reserve air button on the side of his dive mask.

Emergency air 5 min.

He grasped the dive knife and instead of swimming deeper into the tank he crouched down by the driver's chair underneath the opening.

The scorpion's claws instantly appeared as the creature swam forward into the tank two feet above him. As he looked up he saw what he had hoped to see.

The scorpion had an underbelly free of any protective shell. With all the strength he had Maddox thrust the knife up into the scorpion. The steel cut into the scorpion right up to the top of the blade's handle, and Maddox held on tightly hoping to run the knife right across the rest of the underbelly as the scorpion's momentum continued forward.

But the knife barely moved and to Maddox's horror the scorpion's armour like tissue bent the blade. Still wounded the scorpion shot forward in a panic deeper into the tank then up and through the hatch back out into the Nile, leaving a small trail of blood behind, the knife still stuck in its underbelly.

Maddox's dive screen flashed.

Emergency air 4 min.

A whole minute hadn't passed, but Maddox was breathing faster than normal as he fought the scorpion.

Maddox froze in alarm for a split second, realizing he was losing oxygen faster than he expected to and that even steel blades were useless against the creature. He then quickly refocused and swam back up into the plane looking for the torch just as the scorpion reappeared atop the tank's hatch. Once inside the plane he quickly grasped the torch just as the scorpion's black eyes and claws reappeared from inside the tank.

Maddox pressed the trigger and the red flame burst directly in front of the creature's face. The scorpion spun in fear back towards the tank, but as it turned its right claw caught the torch's nozzle, spinning the fiery tool out of Maddox's hand towards the far corner of the plane's midsection near the tail.

Maddox didn't try to recover the torch, knowing he was dead if it was broken and he had cornered himself inside the plane. Instead he rotated and swam through the opening back out into the Nile. After swimming a dozen feet he looked back and saw the scorpion shoot out of the tank's hatch and disappear into the gloom.

Emergency air 3 min.

He waited to see if the scorpion reappeared knowing he would never reach the surface in time if it chased him.

Sure enough after ten seconds the creature reappeared out of the gloom, but instead of appearing near the tank it now swam close to the river's surface. Suddenly it seemed to lock onto Maddox and with a flash of its tail it plunged feverishly down towards him!

Maddox didn't swim back inside the plane's midsection. He didn't swim for the tank either.

Instead he headed for the fighter plane's cockpit.

Hurriedly he swung the canopy open. In one motion he then swam down into the seat as he pulled the canopy closed behind him. Just as he closed it the scorpion appeared and its claws sliced against the canopy causing the entire plane to shake due to the force. Small pieces of glass and steel broke free, but the canopy held and the scorpion turned aside and began to circle the plane.

Emergency air 2 min.

Maddox sat and stared forward thinking furiously about what he could do. He was safe from the scorpion but if he didn't move the air would run out and the cockpit would become his coffin. Certain death if he left the cockpit, certain death if he stayed.

He looked down at the remains of the control stick floating free and then up as the scorpion swam past the plane's propeller. He imagined how great it would be if somehow the guns could fire underwater after all these years, and he could blast the scorpion out of the Nile.

He shifted in the seat and undid the backpack's straps, lifting it onto his lap. He then pulled out the painting and notebook and let the backpack float away against the control panel.

He looked down at the notebook, the dive mask light illuminating the eerie swastika carved into the box lid. He could only guess what secrets Wolfgang had written inside the notebook. But he knew that whatever they were, they would save the lives of people he cared deeply about.

Suddenly the scorpion re-appeared and its right claw scraped against the canopy once again, but with no new result. Maddox didn't even bother to look up at the underwater predator, instead he placed the notebook safely inside the now empty chainsaw holster behind his back, and looked closely at the painting package. Suddenly a wild idea occurred to him and he muttered,

"Sorry Randel."

He then began to rip the package to pieces until he held the torn painting in his hands, the light illuminating the rich canvas which featured the aforementioned camel and jackal fighting each other in the heart of a sandstorm. Near the centre of the painting was a large tear, a bullet hole. And to the right of the bullet hole was a much larger jagged slash in the canvas.

He then turned the painting over. No exit tear of any kind. The bullet was still inside. Maddox then placed both hands against each side of the larger tear and ripped the painting completely open...to reveal two serrated daggers, each a foot long and covered in a thin coating of gold.

Emergency air 1 min.

Maddox looked closely at the daggers, seeing that much of the gold was missing on the front of both blades but not on the back sides. It looked as if the gold had been recently and roughly scraped off. He looked closer and could see the bullet lying at the bottom of the painting's outer rim. The bullet was warped and twisted out of the shape, while the daggers weren't even bent.

He looked up in shock suddenly realizing that the scorpion's stinger hadn't missed the daggers, but had in fact been *stopped* when it hit the gold covered steel of each blade. The daggers had stopped the stinger from continuing forward and going straight through his back, just as one of them had stopped a modern bullet with ease more than a week before.

He let go of the painting and lifted both daggers, surprised at the weight and at the intricately carved white handles that appeared to have been made out of marble. He had expected the blades to literally disintegrate in the water due to Amber's tablet readings. He now knew why Randel was willing to pay millions to recover them. Whatever their age, these weren't ordinary blades made of steel. They were made of something else...something almost indestructible.

He had seconds before the air ran out.

He needed to get close to slice the underbelly. The creature's thick skin wouldn't bend these blades. But facing the scorpion head on seemed close to suicide out in the open water. He thought about possibly luring it back into the tank where he could wait to strike somewhat protected, or wait in the plane and hope the scorpion came close enough to the cockpit again. But then his dive screen flashed:

Emergency air 0 min.

The air was gone.

With no other choice left Maddox left the painting in the cockpit and opened the canopy. Then seeing the scorpion circle the plane's tail, he swam out with a dagger in each hand to meet it.

Keeping the plane close to his left hand he didn't wait and kicked his feet to speed up. He could only hold his breath for so long and didn't have time to waste.

The scorpion saw him and swung its tail back and forth to increase speed and in two seconds they were upon each other. The scorpion immediately recoiled its tail and stinger while Maddox instinctively hunched down beside the plane's fuselage just as the stinger shot forward towards him. Maddox ducked his head even further and the black barb missed his head by four inches above and to the right. Before the creature could pull the stinger free of the plane's steel Maddox dove forward inches above the Nile's mud bottom until he was directly underneath the scorpion's underbelly.

With a yell he then drove both daggers up and into the creature's innards. The scorpion immediately spun free before he could slice the creature completely open. The stinger was pulled free and the scorpion rotated up and to the left to prepare to attack Maddox from above.

Maddox looked up in amazement at the scorpion's speed. With one flash of its tail it had repositioned itself a dozen feet above him in a split second, and he had nowhere to hide before the next stinger attack.

But then the crocodiles came.

Smelling the scorpion's blood in the water, the other top predators of the Nile had joined the fight.

Two large crocodiles swam furiously over the Nazi plane's propeller before splitting in two different directions. One sunk its jaws into the scorpion's side while the other swam down and beneath the scorpion...to seize Maddox.

He spun to his left as the ancient predator snapped its jaws missing him. He reached up and grasped the crocodiles back with his left hand to hold on, while he plunged the dagger in his right into the side of the crocodile's neck.

The beast snapped its head back as far as it could, but Maddox was out of its reach. He then spun lower and stabbed the underside of the crocodile's throat. In desperation the beast shook to throw Maddox off and Maddox lost his grip and floated backwards and down. The crocodile swung back and snapped one last time at Maddox, its last act before dying. All Maddox saw were the jaws rushing towards his face, then the white jagged teeth as they bit into his mask before pulling back for good.

Maddox opened his eyes to realize the crocodile hadn't bit through the mask all the way to his face, but had savagely punctured the left side of the mask's goggles. Had Maddox been wearing a regular dive mask and not his own special reinforced model, the crocodile would have torn his face off. But with half of the dive mask now cracked and broken, Maddox could only see out of the right side.

As the mortally wounded crocodile swam away Maddox looked back up towards the plane hoping to see the other Nile crocodile had killed the underwater "arachnid." Instead the two creatures were still fighting to the death and the crocodile had bitten down on one of the scorpion's curved claws, savagely trying to rip it off while spinning over and over in the water as it held on.

But suddenly the spinning stopped as the stinger flashed and went straight through the crocodile's midsection and out the other side. The crocodile let go of the half chewed claw, paralyzed and dying.

Maddox didn't wait for the scorpion to pull the stinger out, instead he instinctively kicked his fins and swam upward, grasped the dying crocodile with one hand and slashing at the scorpion's tail near the stinger with the other.

The serrated dagger cut through the tail with ease and the scorpion flung backwards in fear and pain, as the now dead crocodile floated away with the scorpion's bonelike stinger still stuck in its back.

As the scorpion disappeared back inside the plane, Maddox placed both daggers into the leg sheath as he began to involuntarily cough.

He knew he was beginning to drown.

All he had to do now was reach the surface.

With his hands now completely free he pulled himself upward through the water towards the yacht, reminding himself as the Egyptian daylight grew clearer with every stroke:

It's only twenty feet...it's only ten feet...it's only five....it's only...

He suddenly stopped as what vision he had left through the mask began to go black. He was going unconscious and as he fought the sensation he realized he was also being pulled back down into the depths of the Nile.

Turning he saw the scorpion had followed him one last time, and had its hideous claws grasping each of his legs.

He turned back to fight but as he was going unconscious he couldn't even find the knives strapped to his leg, his mind now too unclear to function correctly.

As he was pulled down the last thing he saw through the cracked dive mask was the faint image of two divers swimming towards him...and then he heard something that sounded strangely like a chainsaw.

As Maddox slumped unresponsively Travis and Amber reached him and the scorpion, each carrying their own underwater chainsaw. Without haste they attacked the creature, cutting off each of its claws with ease. Now completely paralyzed and bleeding heavily the amphibious creature spun backwards and disappeared down into the murky waters of the Nile for good.

Maddox's two best friends then carried him to the top as quickly as possible breaking the surface to gasps and cheers on the yacht. In seconds Maddox was laid out on the deck where Amber performed C.P.R. on him.

Maddox quickly came to and roughly spit out the river water while coughing fiercely. Finally okay he then looked up at his two friends and said, "Aren't those chainsaws awesome?"

They just laughed until Maddox asked seriously.

"Is the scorpion dead?"

Travis responded, "Dead or dying."

Maddox then noticed that both Amber and Travis were wearing steel handcuffs but with the chains broken. "What's with the cuffs?"

Amber replied, "When you dove over the rail we decided that we had to go too. But once we got the gear we needed, the kindly Officer here noticed and had us arrested and put in handcuffs and placed in one of the yacht's cabins...which turned out to be our supplies room."

Travis lifted the broken cuffs and smiled directly at the Officer in charge, "Which also contained our chainsaws!"

The Officer showed the barest hint of a smile while still answering coldly, "I can still have you arrested for multiple charges."

Maddox slowly stood and shielded his eyes from the sunlight with one hand before anyone got a glimpse of his eyes. He then spoke to the Officer, "Don't worry man, the scorpion will never hurt anyone again. And all three of us are finished with the Nile."

The Officer looked at him intensely.

"And you actually mean it this time??"

Maddox nodded and pointed to his friends who beamed at his words, "We achieved everything here we wanted to."

The Officer in charge finally smiled for real and he curtly shook hands with the Treasure Rebels. "In that case charges are dropped, but you three will need to give statements at our station to ensure the thieves are prosecuted properly...say in three hours?"

"We'll be there, man."

The Officer then ordered his men to prepare the police boats to sail for shore. As the police were leaving the deck Amber handed Maddox the copper sunglasses while Randel and Victor stepped forward anxiously to speak.

Randel was shocked, never having seen anyone look the way Maddox did. His dive suit was torn in multiple places, his legs and face were bleeding, and in his hand was the dive mask, cracked and smashed. Yet the expression on Maddox's face along with the sunglasses made him look as if he was as relaxed as a surfer who was chilling on a beach.

"I had no idea all these terrible things would happen to any of you! Thank you, all of you, for what you risked."

He then paused and looked at the Officer slowly descending the ladder onto the police cruiser. "You told that man that you achieved everything you wanted. Does that mean you have the painting on you strapped to your dive suit?"

Maddox grinned. "No, it's still down there."

Randel almost fainted, but after quickly composing himself grunted, "We had a deal and now that the scorpion is dead you must return to retrieve my-"

Maddox cut him off by pulling the daggers out of the leg sheath, the sun glistening off the shimmering white blades.

Randel was speechless as Maddox handed the unique weapons over to him.

After studying the blades for a full ten seconds Randel finally said, "I APOLIGIZE for misleading you three about the painting!! In essence though I was truthful, these daggers are artwork in themselves and are ornamental in nature only! They would be absolutely useless in actual combat."

Maddox adjusted the sunglasses on his face a little and did his best to keep from smiling at Randel's weak attempt at misleading them.

"You're the art expert Mr. King."

EPILOGUE

The Treasure Rebels stood calmly and relaxed against a rail with the Great Sphinx in the distance behind them, relaxing and laughing as they drank ice cold water and pop. They were wearing the same clothes when they had first landed in Egypt more than a week ago, and to all the tourists walking past they looked like average Americans who had taken a break from exploring the Giza pyramids because of the excruciating Egyptian heat.

In reality they were waiting to be paid three million dollars.

Ten minutes later every tourist suddenly stopped what they were doing to look into the distance, half stunned by what they saw. Out of the heat waves and dust came the Rolls Royce Phantom, slowly pulling to a stop in front of the Rebels.

At the wheel was Randel with Victor riding shotgun, while their two girlfriends who were both Hollywood actresses rode in the backseat while watching a tennis match on the large flat screen tv.

Both businessmen jumped out onto the dirt and walked up to the Rebels with huge smiles on their faces. In Randel's right hand was a brown business satchel.

They all shook hands and Randel happily handed the satchel to Maddox.

"Here it is as promised! Three million dollars, the finest money I've spent in a long time. You crazy young adventurers earned every single dollar!"

Maddox didn't even open the satchel, instead he handed it to Amber and Travis who quickly opened and analyzed the three cheques all made out to one million dollars. Amber pulled out another tablet computer and placed the three cheques on the screen. With the push of a button the cheques were slowly scanned.

Meanwhile Maddox looked off into the distance lost in thought. Victor noticed and slapped Maddox on the back while saying, "Dreaming of what you're going to do with all that money I bet!!"

Maddox replaced Wolfgang's notebook in his back pocket unnoticed and replied, "Actually man, I was thinkin' about the next adventure."

Amber looked up from the tablet and thanked Randel. "The money is certainly all good!"

Behind them one of the businessmen's girlfriends called out, "Randel, we have to hurry, the movie shoot starts in an hour!"

Randel turned to his business partner. "Can you tell them I'll be just another minute?"

"Of course!"

Victor waved goodbye to the Rebels and cheerfully went back to the Phantom, happy for the opportunity to continue flirting with his girlfriend.

Randel turned back to the adventurers, his expression suddenly serious yet also grateful.

"I want to thank you personally for diving in the face of such danger. Very courageous! Most would have ignored my plea and the daggers would still be trapped in the Nile for who knows how long! I want you to know how much your bravery means to me."

He then extended his hand to Travis saying, "I want to also shake your hand and thank you personally Mr. Jagson for saving my life on the yacht. I can't express what your bravery means to me."

Travis shook his hand replying simply, "You're welcome."

Randel then shook Amber's hand saying, "Thank you as well for your help in capturing those crooks on my yacht. Without your help who knows what would have happened to everyone."

Amber shook his hand and replied sincerely, "You're most welcome Mr. King."

Randel then pointed to the satchel saying, "You can keep the satchel if you want, but if you don't I'll just take it now and be on my way."

But instead of the satchel Amber handed him a white envelope.

"We want you to know that we know everything first."

Randel looked at the envelope questioningly and opening it he began to study the pages it contained.

As he read Amber stated, "That is a photocopy of fifteen pages from a diary written by a French soldier in Napoleon's army, Gregory King. His brother was the artist Miguel King, and he wrote how together they planned to win favour with the French Dictator by giving him two rare gifts, a special dagger from each of them. Miguel wanted to become one of France's most popular artists, while Gregory wanted a promotion. According to Gregory he was something of an archaeologist before joining the military, and he claimed to have found fossilized teeth of a sabre-tooth tiger or some other ancient predator. He couldn't have been much of an archaeologist, because he suggested to Miguel that they contact a local blacksmith and use the large teeth as handles for the pair of daggers.

"He doesn't explain how but he writes that Miguel was wealthy and that the blacksmith forged the blades from diamonds Miguel owned along with a rare metal. As an added bonus the handles were layered in a thin coating of marble. He doesn't give any details how the blacksmith would create such blades. After paying the blacksmith a large sum they tested the daggers claiming that they were better than any blades the army currently used. But before they could arrange an audience with Napoleon, the little Dictator left Egypt, and they were completely stuck. Gregory had been assigned to another country and Miguel would travel back to France. They thought it would be too dangerous to carry the daggers with them, and they didn't want to separate the blades either. So they decided to hide the daggers in a painting which Miguel hurriedly sketched hours before they had to leave. He apparently admitted it wasn't his best work and that he didn't care at all for it"

Travis looked at Maddox and grinned, "So I guess if he were still around he wouldn't care the painting was destroyed and left inside a fighter plane underwater."

Amber continued, "The painting went with Miguel and he tried for years to get an audience with Napoleon, but he never had any success. Miguel eventually died from Typhus years later in 1813, and he had the painting given to Gregory in his will. Gregory survived the Napoleonic Wars, but once Napoleon was defeated for good in 1815 Gregory knew the dream was over. So much for your "legend" that the painting hung in Napoleon's private quarters. The painting and daggers became a family secret, and the painting was passed down from generation to generation until it became yours Mr. King. The whole diary is in Cairo's largest library, took me three days of searching to find it, but we scribbled the call number on the first page of those photocopies in case you want to see the rest of it."

Maddox spoke directly at Randel who sheepishly continued reading the diary pages without looking up.

"You should have told us what the real treasure was all along."

Travis handed back the satchel and said, "We won't say a word because we know you're the rightful owner of the daggers. We just don't like being lied to."

Randel sighed in relief, "I apologize to you three. I felt being treasure hunters you would search for the painting but would laugh off the idea of sabre-tooth daggers with blades made of diamonds as impossible."

Travis then asked him, "What about the Vultures? You must have known there were criminals out to rob you."

Randel wiped his brow more out of anxiety than trying to wipe the perspiration away and answered, "I admit I knew I was a target for thieves for a long time, but I honestly did not know of the mercenaries with Uzis. The police pulled the remains of the diver who died a week ago, and they have contacted his family. It appears the entire gang are some sort of international mercenaries, and as we speak they are being extradited back to their home countries. As for the thief who actually robbed me and his accomplice in the boat, there is no evidence they were linked to the ones who attacked my yacht. The mercenaries must have overheard in the Cairo underworld about my trying to hire help to retrieve the painting and decided to rob me themselves."

"I think you might want to be more discreet in the future when speaking about your collection in public."

Randel nodded his head in agreement.

"I agree Miss Monette. I see that now."

He then quickly changed the topic to the scorpion.

"The scientists pulled the remains of the creature out of the Nile four days ago. They studied it and declared that it is indeed a new type of species never seen before. They believe it is a surviving relative of the Eurypterids, known as Sea Scorpions, which lived eons ago. Except this "scorpion" had a tail far more dangerous than its prehistoric relatives. The authorities are searching the Nile as we speak but thankfully all signs point to it being the only one in the river. They haven't figured out why it came up the Nile or where it came from. They haven't even given it a name yet."

Randel then looked back at the limousine eager to get going but continued, "Before you leave, there will be plenty of reporters at the airport who will ask you for a statement. Since the creature has no official name you might want to simply refer to it as the scorpion or creature."

"We'll give the reporters a more accurate name than that Randel."

Randel looked at Maddox questionably.

"How so?"

"We'll just tell them we killed a dinosaur."

Randel just chuckled and began saying goodbye to each of them.

But when he came to Maddox last he asked, "I hate to be rude, but I've wanted to ask from the beginning...why do you wear those strange sunglasses all the time?"

Maddox looked straight ahead.

"Shark bite."

Randel shook his head and laughed replying, "Okay, I won't ask again. I admit I will miss your sense of humour."

"I'm not kiddin' man. I was bitten by a blue shark in the Mediterranean Sea over two months ago right through the mask. My eyes weren't injured, but the skin around my eyes and forehead were damaged pretty bad. The doctors examined the bite and say I can still dive, but I don't want anybody to see my face for now."

Randel shook Maddox's hand and simply nodded his head, not believing a single word. He finally walked away towards the idling car while calling back to all three of them, "Enjoy the money!"

He then got behind the wheel and honking the horn he happily sped away towards Cairo, while one of the actresses in the back seat made sure to wave goodbye to Maddox and Travis, much to the chagrin of Victor.

Both adventurers waved back to the hot blonde while Travis said, "Funny how he thinks we risked our lives for money. He still thinks we're just adrenaline junkies looking for a rush or run of the mill treasure hunters looking for a huge payday."

With the car now gone Maddox pulled Wolfgang's notebook out of his pocket and began flipping through the pages. "We only dove because it was life or death that we get this. We couldn't wait any longer. People's lives depend on it."

The three Rebels then sat down in the sand and Maddox handed the book to his two best friends.

"Wolfgang was an even bigger genius than we thought."

Travis briefly looked the notebook over for the hundredth time, quickly scanning the torn yellowed pages and the leather cover.

He then handed it to Amber saying, "It still gives me the creeps to hold onto anything a Nazi wrote."

As she looked through the pages she replied, "He describes over forty different locations over a ten year period, often contradicting dates and chronological order. I doubt some of these places even exist."

Maddox slowly finished the rest of the iced pop and answered, "Your right, I think half the book is just fiction from Wolfgang's mind, deliberately trying to mislead anyone who found it."

Amber closed the book and handed it back to Maddox. "Then how can we tell where he found the medicine?"

"Because there's only one place he describes that fits all the pieces."

Suddenly they looked up at the sound of a car horn, and saw the Phantom limo racing back towards them with a cloud of desert sand and dust flying behind the back wheels. Finally it stopped mere feet in front of them. The driver's window smoothly opened and Randel leaned out of the car beaming.

"There is something else I have to say! I admit I became something of a fan when I read about your adventures in the papers. I wanted to ask you...where are you headed for your next adventure?"

With the notebook hidden from view Maddox answered, "Another river."

To his side Travis groaned, "Not another river!"

"Which one?"

"The Congo!"

Randel put the car back in drive and replied, "Looking for more treasure I'm sure!"

Maddox ever so slowly took off the copper tinted sunglasses, revealing two sharp blue eyes surrounded by ugly damaged tissue from the shark bite, and smiling he looked directly at Randel.

"Something even better."

Don't miss out!

Visit the website below and you can sign up to receive emails whenever Gerard Doris publishes a new book. There's no charge and no obligation.

https://books2read.com/r/B-A-WRCD-QDXK

BOOKS 2 READ

Connecting independent readers to independent writers.

Did you love *Nile River Scorpion*? Then you should read *Congo Spider Fangs*[1] by Gerard Doris!

[2]

When a helicopter carrying medicine crashes into a waterfall along the Congo River, the Treasure Rebels are asked to help recover the anti-toxin.

The team accepts the challenge unaware of the wild dangers they are about to face. With no weapons or equipment to protect themselves they must overcome two menacing predators. One waiting in the jungle to hijack their rescue operation. The other an exotic and lethal species of spider not seen by mankind for over 70 years. "Congo Spider Fangs" is the second adventure

---

1. https://books2read.com/u/49x6V0

2. https://books2read.com/u/49x6V0

in the Treasure Rebels novella series, and directly follows the exciting events of "Nile River Scorpion."

Read more at https://gerarddoristhrillers.com.

Also by Gerard Doris

Treasure Rebels Adventure Novella
Nile River Scorpion
Congo Spider Fangs
Amazon Swamp Victory
India Yeti Pirates
Greek Gladiator Sharks

Standalone
Wrath of the Renegades

Watch for more at https://gerarddoristhrillers.com.

About the Author

Thanks for reading! I write adventure fiction that features treasure hunters, pirates, and renegades. I'm also a fan of NFL football, westerns, classic action movies, and anything that promotes genuine adventure. For some fun updates on my writing projects, you can follow me on X (formerly Twitter) at: @gerard_advfict

Read more at https://gerarddoristhrillers.com.